# Hide-and-Seek Turkeys

BY JUDITH ROSS ENDERLE
AND
STEPHANIE JACOB GORDON

ILLUSTRATED BY TERESA MURFIN

Margaret K. McElderry Books
New York   London   Toronto   Sydney

Ten turkeys
played hide-and-seek,
till . . .

the fox
showed
up,
sneak, sneak, sneak.

Turkeys flapped two by two.
Into the farmer's house they flew,
where . . .

one turkey
hid under a wig.

One more came and she was much too big.

There was not enough room! Not enough room for two turkeys under that wig.

So . . .

two turkeys hid
    in high-button shoes until . . .

one more came and got bad news.

There was not enough room! Not enough room
    for three turkeys
        in high-button shoes.

So . . .

three turkeys hid in a tricorn hat until . . .

one more came and that was that!

There was not enough room! Not enough room
for four turkeys in a tricorn hat.

So . . .

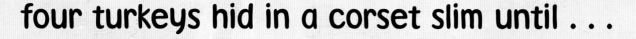

four turkeys hid in a corset slim until . . .

one more came and they said to him,

"There is not enough room! Not enough room
for five turkeys in a corset slim."

So . . .

five turkeys hid in some britches round.
One more came and it was found,

there was not enough room!
Not enough room

for six turkeys
in those britches round.
So . . .

six turkeys hid 'neath a petticoat wide until . . .

one more came to get inside. But . . .

there was not enough room! Not enough room

for seven turkeys 'neath a petticoat wide.

So . . .

seven turkeys hid in a waistcoat red until . . .

one more came and the others said,

"There is not enough room! Not enough room for eight turkeys in this waistcoat red."

So . . .

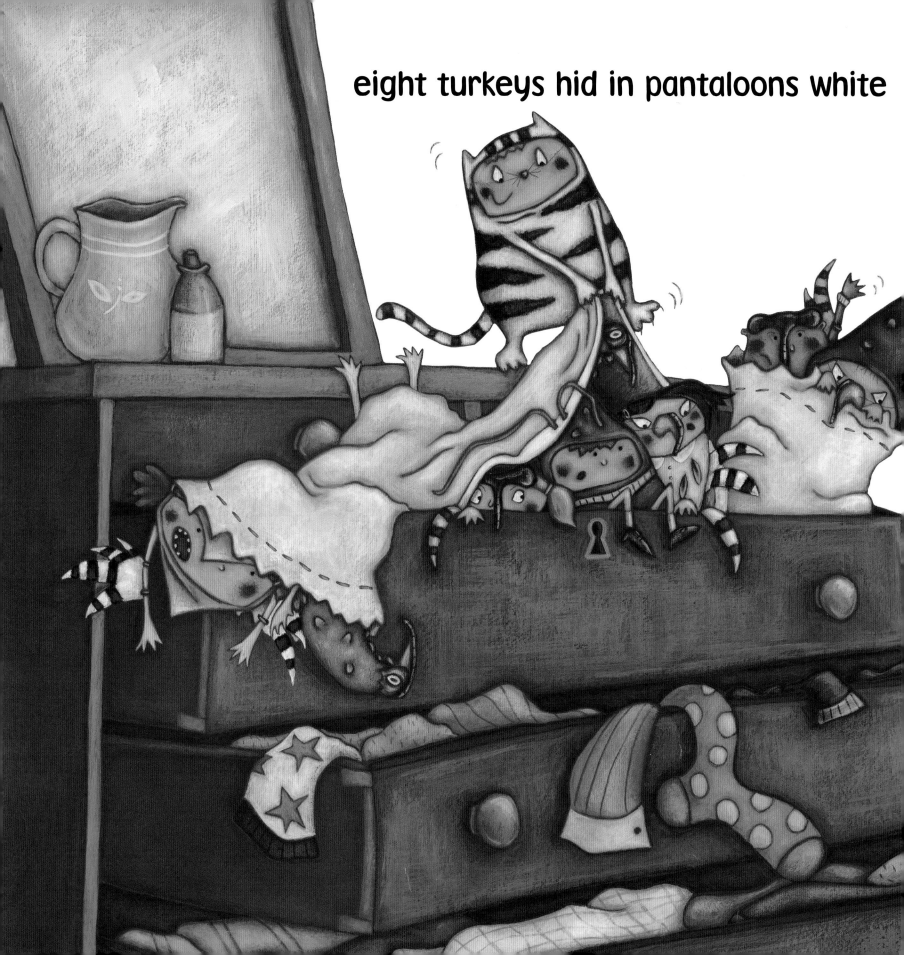

eight turkeys hid in pantaloons white

until . . .

one more came and it was just too tight. For . . .

there was not enough room! Not enough room

for nine turkeys

in pantaloons white.

So . . .

nine turkeys hid
in the farmer's
wife's frocks.
One more came
and squawk-ity squawked, as . . .

ready or not, along came the fox
and . . .

there was
not enough room!
Not enough room
for even one fox
in the farmer's wife's frocks.

So turkeys flapped
and turkeys flew,

just as the farmer
came inside.

And they did!

# They hid!

1, 2, 3, 4, 5, 6, 7, 8, 9, 10!

For our clever little turkeys—
Sam, Sarah, Talya Rose, Lily, Zoey, Hannah, and Jacob
—J. R. E. and S. J. G.

For Tom, Mum, and Dad
—T. M.

Margaret K. McElderry Books
An imprint of Simon & Schuster Children's Publishing Division
1230 Avenue of the Americas, New York, New York 10020
Text copyright © 2004 by Judith Ross Enderle and Stephanie Jacob Gordon
Illustrations copyright © 2004 by Teresa Murfin
The text for this book is set in Fontoon.
The illustrations for this book are rendered in acrylic on board.
Manufactured in China
2 4 6 8 10 9 7 5 3 1
Library of Congress Cataloging-in-Publication Data
Enderle, Judith Ross.
Hide-and-seek turkeys / Judith Ross Enderle and Stephanie Jacob Gordon ; illustrated by Teresa Murfin.
p. cm.
Summary: Children perform a school play about ten turkeys that hide in the farmer's house from a fox.
ISBN 0-689-84715-7
[1. Theater—Fiction. 2. Schools—Fiction. 3. Turkeys—Fiction. 4. Foxes—Fiction. 5. Counting—Fiction.
6. Stories in rhyme.] I. Gordon, Stephanie Jacob, 1940- II. Murfin, Teresa, ill. III. Title.
PZ8.3.E557 Hi 2004
[E]—dc21
2002006186

FIRST
EDITION